Our Favourite Rhymes

Illustrated by David McKee

Contents

Little Miss Muffet

Little Miss Muffet
sat on a tuffet,
eating her curds and whey.
There came a big spider
who sat down beside her
and frightened Miss Muffet away.

Hickory dickory dock

Hickory dickory dock,
the mouse ran up the clock,
the clock struck one,
the mouse ran down,
Hickory dickory dock.

Little Jack Horner

Little Jack Horner
sat in a corner,
eating a Christmas pie.
He put in his thumb
and pulled out a plum,
and said, "What a good boy am I!"

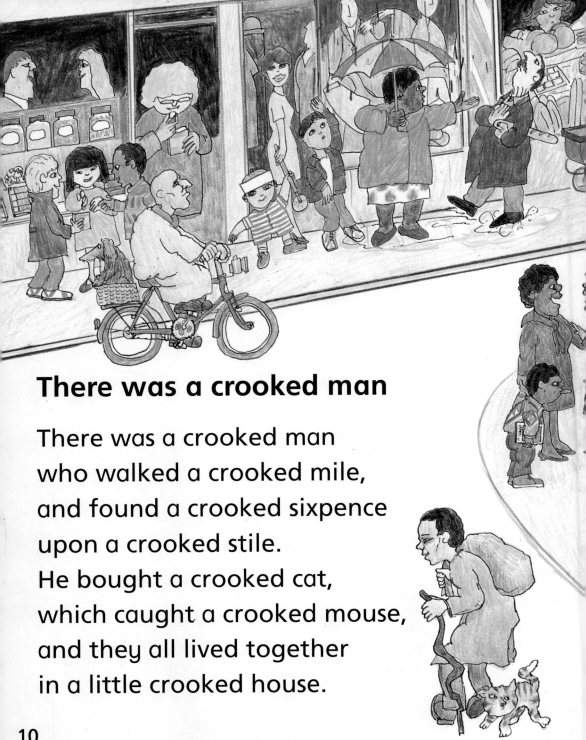

There was a crooked man

There was a crooked man
who walked a crooked mile,
and found a crooked sixpence
upon a crooked stile.
He bought a crooked cat,
which caught a crooked mouse,
and they all lived together
in a little crooked house.

Humpty Dumpty

Humpty Dumpty sat on a wall,
Humpty Dumpty had a great fall.
All the king's horses and all the king's men
couldn't put Humpty together again.

13

Pussy cat, pussy cat

"Pussy cat, pussy cat,
where have you been?"

"I've been to London
to look at the Queen."

"Pussy cat, pussy cat,
what did you there?"

"I frightened a little mouse
under her chair."

Twinkle, twinkle little star

Twinkle, twinkle little star,
how I wonder what you are!
Up above the world so high,
like a diamond in the sky.

The grand old Duke of York

The grand old Duke of York,
he had ten thousand men,
he marched them up to the top of the hill
and he marched them down again!

And when they were up they were up,
and when they were down they were down,
and when they were only half way up,
they were neither up nor down.

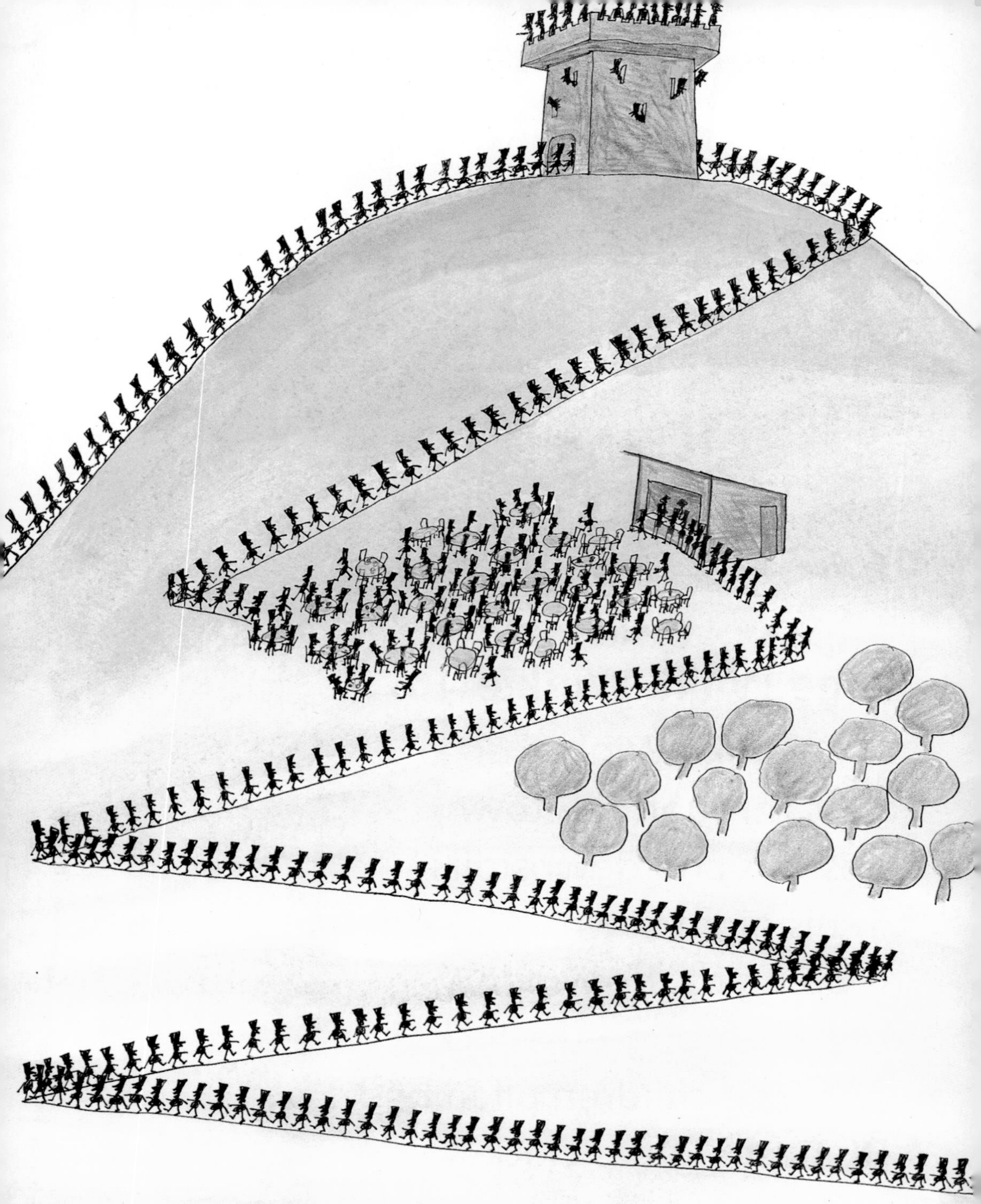

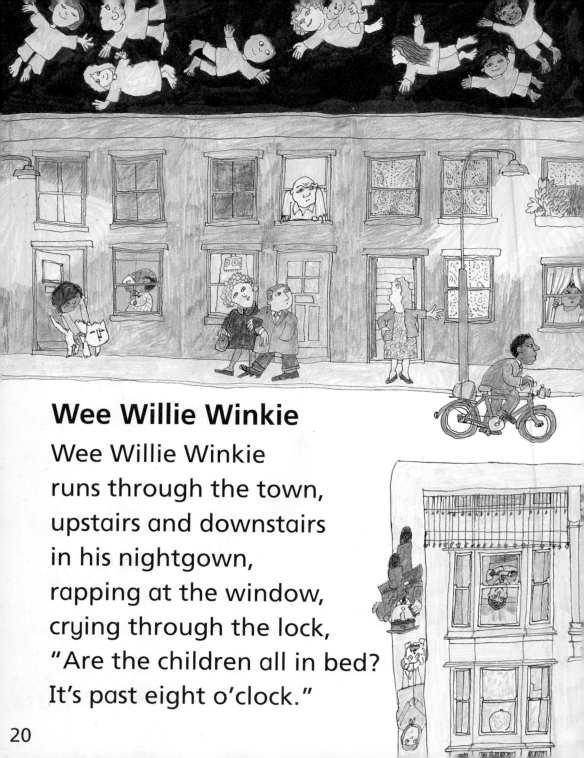

Wee Willie Winkie

Wee Willie Winkie
runs through the town,
upstairs and downstairs
in his nightgown,
rapping at the window,
crying through the lock,
"Are the children all in bed?
It's past eight o'clock."

Sing a song of sixpence

Sing a song of sixpence,
a pocket full of rye,
four and twenty blackbirds
baked in a pie.

When the pie was opened,
the birds began to sing.
Wasn't that a dainty dish
to set before the king?

The king was in his counting-house
counting out his money.
The queen was in the parlour
eating bread and honey.

The maid was in the garden
hanging out the clothes,
when down came a blackbird
and pecked off her nose!

23

Mary, Mary quite contrary

"Mary, Mary quite contrary,
how does your garden grow?"

"With silver bells and cockle-shells
and pretty maids all in a row."

Jack and Jill went up the hill

Jack and Jill went up the hill
to fetch a pail of water,
Jack fell down and broke his crown
and Jill came tumbling after.

26

Hey diddle diddle

Hey diddle diddle,
the cat and the fiddle,
the cow jumped over the moon.
The little dog laughed to see such fun,
and the dish ran away with the spoon.

This book is part of

THE LONGMAN BOOK PROJECT

General Editor Sue Palmer
Fiction Editor Wendy Body
Non-fiction Editor Bobbie Neate

ADDISON WESLEY LONGMAN LIMITED
Edinburgh Gate, Harlow, Essex, CM20 2JE, England and Associated
Companies throughout the World.

Illustrations © David McKee

First published 1994
Third impression 1998
ISBN 0 582 12087 X
Also available in larger format ISBN 0 582 12079 9
Set in Lefrut 33/47 pt.
Printed in Singapore through Addison Wesley Longman China Limited

The publisher's policy is to use paper manufactured from sustainable forests.